T0196816

A
KNIGHT
IN THE VILLE

A
KNIGHT
IN THE VILLE

The Diary

Steven E. Winters

authorHOUSE®

AuthorHouse™
1663 Liberty Drive
Bloomington, IN 47403
www.authorhouse.com
Phone: 1 (800) 839-8640

© 2015 Steven E. Winters. All rights reserved.

No part of this book may be reproduced, stored in a retrieval system, or transmitted by any means without the written permission of the author.

Published by AuthorHouse   08/21/2015

ISBN: 978-1-5049-3232-5 (sc)
ISBN: 978-1-5049-3233-2 (e)

Library of Congress Control Number: 2015913524

Print information available on the last page.

Any people depicted in stock imagery provided by Thinkstock are models, and such images are being used for illustrative purposes only. Certain stock imagery © Thinkstock.

This book is printed on acid-free paper.

Because of the dynamic nature of the Internet, any web addresses or links contained in this book may have changed since publication and may no longer be valid. The views expressed in this work are solely those of the author and do not necessarily reflect the views of the publisher, and the publisher hereby disclaims any responsibility for them.

"I wish I could show you the little village where I was born. It's so lovely there…I used to think it too small to spend a life in, but now I'm not so sure."

Mary Kelly

CHAPTER ONE

The crackling voice on the radio came just as Curtis Knight was raising a spoonful of chili to his mouth. "Tyler dispatch calling Sistersville Unit 100."

Grabbing his walkie-talkie, he responded, "This is Sistersville Unit 100. Go ahead, dispatch."

"Please respond to a domestic disturbance at the Sky Williams residence on North Main Street. Caller reports two females fighting in the front yard."

Curtis shook his head and sighed. It never failed … he *always* got a call when he sat down for dinner! "Ten-four! I'm on my way!"

Rising from the kitchen table, he placed the bowl in the fridge and walked outside to his patrol car. He jumped inside and fired the Ford up, not bothering with the lights and siren since the Williams house was only a few blocks away. As he rounded the diamond square at the city building that separated north and south Main Streets, he recognized the two females ahead and winced.

It was Erin and Sharon Harris, also known as the Harris twins.

Curtis pulled over on the opposite side of the street from the Williams house and shut off his cruiser. He jumped out and ran over to the sisters, who were standing on the sidewalk, screaming obscenities at each other. "Whoa! Whoa! That's enough! The next one of you who screams is going to jail!"

The sisters stopped screaming and took a step away from each other as Curtis got in between them. "Erin, I want you to go stand by the back of my cruiser while I talk to your sister. When I'm finished getting her side of the story, I'll talk to you. Now go!"

Erin lowered her head sheepishly and walked across the street to the cruiser. "Now, Sharon, you just have a seat on the curb here and tell me what in the world you two are fighting about."

Sharon pulled her auburn hair back from her face and slowly sat down. "I was just here visitin' my man, and she comes runnin' up here with her mouth flappin', talkin' all 'kinda of shit."

"Let's keep the language civil, okay? That ugly word doesn't sit well coming from the mouth of such a pretty young lady."

Sharon blushed and murmured softly, "Sorry."

"That's okay. Now let's start over."

"I was here seein' Sky. We been datin' 'bout a week now, and Erin caught wind of it and is tryin' to stir stuff up. She used to date him, but they broke up, and now she's jealous."

Curtis nodded and took out his notepad. "Where is Sky?"

"He ran inside when she pulled up."

Curtis chuckled and jotted down a few lines before closing the notepad. "You can go on inside the house, Sharon. I'm going to talk to your sister."

Sharon nodded and stood, casting a glare in the direction of her sister before marching up the front steps onto Sky's front porch. She pulled on the front door, but it would not open. Just then, a window opened on the second floor, and Sky Williams leaned out. "Hey, Curtis! I want both of these crazy women off my property ... NOW!"

Sharon stepped off the porch and looked up at Sky. "Baby, let me in!

"No! I'm done with you, Sharon. It's over! You and your crazy sister are too much drama for me! Don't ever come back!"

Sharon burst into tears, and within a few seconds, Erin was racing across the street to hug and comfort her. "How dare you dump my sister like this, Sky Williams? You're an asshole!"

"Yes, I am! Now get off my property, and don't neither of you ever come back!"

Curtis walked over to the sisters and patted Erin on the shoulder. "It's time to go. Since he instructed you in my presence not to return to his property, if either of you come back here, I'll have to arrest you for trespassing."

"Don't worry about that, Officer! Neither of us will *ever* be coming back here! Come on, Sharon."

After the sisters left, Curtis looked up. "Sky, come downstairs and let me in."

While he waited for Sky to open the front door, Curtis shook his head. The Harris twins were notorious in the area for fighting over the same men. Some of the local folks referred to them as "Erin and Sharin'" because whenever one girl developed an interest in a man, the other one wanted him, too. At twenty-three years of age, both girls stood about 5'7" and were blessed with pretty faces, fine bodies, and long, flowing red hair. Their only flaw was that they were both plumb crazy. Curtis hoped that they would return to their Doddridge County farm and stay there.

The front door opened a few inches, and Sky Williams peeked through the crack before opening it completely. "Come on in, Curtis! Sorry about all this. I guess all the stories about those gals are true!"

"Like you didn't know that," Curtis mumbled as he pushed past Sky and entered the house.

"Oh come on, Curtis! Can you blame me? I mean, they're freaking *twins*! Isn't that every guy's fantasy?"

"I've found that fantasy and reality don't mix well, Sky. But I do get it. Still, when you play with fire …"

Sky laughed and finished his sentence, "… you get burned! Have a seat, old friend. Can I get you a soda pop or some sweet iced tea?"

"That sounds good. Go light on the ice and heavy on the sweet."

As Sky headed to the kitchen, Curtis sat down on the sofa and picked up a copy of his friend's novel, which was sitting on the coffee table. After graduating from high school in Sistersville, Sky had moved to North Carolina, where he had written articles for several magazines and had some poetry published. But this was his first novel—*Inside the Great Minds of History*—and it had catapulted Sky Williams into the national limelight. The book had risen to number three on *The New York Times*

Best Sellers list and had remained in the top ten for six months. After selling the movie rights to Hollywood, Sky had recently returned to the Ville a rich man.

"Here you go, Curtis. Heavy on the sugar," Sky said as he handed Curtis a large, frosty mug.

"Sky, I haven't had a chance to hang out with you since you moved back. But I was hoping it would be under better circumstances."

"Amen to that! We've come a long way since high school, eh? Now here you are, the chief of police! That's awesome."

"Kind of pales in comparison to being a famous writer, but yeah, I'm a pretty big deal here."

Both men laughed and spent the next hour reminiscing, before Curtis started to feel hunger pangs. He was anxious to get home and warm up that delicious chili Amy had made him.

"Don't be a stranger, Curtis. Drop by anytime."

"I will, Sky. And remember, reality and fantasy don't mix!"

After Curtis left, Sky closed the front door. He walked over to the coffee table and picked up his book. *Oh how very wrong you are, Curtis,* he thought as a twisted smile formed on his lips.

CHAPTER TWO

Jessica Long pulled her silver Lexus into her parents' driveway on McCoy Heights just after 1:00 a.m. The porch light came on, and the back door opened. John Long came out of the house and walked over to her car.

"Hello, Daddy!"

"Jess, we need to talk. Before you start to unpack, I need to know: are you here to make amends with your mother, or do you have another agenda?"

Jessica pretended to pout and decided to turn on the waterworks. She knew her father would give in to her. He always did. "Daddy, I've missed you so much!" The tears were faker than her eyelashes, but they flowed easily when she wanted them to.

"I can't stand raising my son without you in his life. He needs a role model, and you're the best man for that job. I *need* you, Daddy. *He* needs you!" Jessica turned the faucets on full blast. Her father opened her car door and leaned in. He then wrapped his arms around her and gave her a strong hug.

"I never doubted you, baby girl. But your mom … well, she …"

"I know, Daddy. But that's my fault. I pushed Mom away. I just want to come home and be your little girl again. I want us to be a family."

While her father carried her suitcases inside the house, Jessica unbuckled her son's car seat. He had slept for most of the trip, which had taken nearly eleven hours. Jessica looked at his face and smiled. *You look exactly like your father. There's no way he could deny you!*

"Everything is in your room, and I set up your old cradle for the boy earlier tonight."

"Thank you! Is Mom up?"

"Yes, but she's not feeling up to seeing you right now. Just give her some time, Jess. She does love you. Good night."

Jessica gave her father a hug and kissed him on the cheek. She took a few cans of baby formula from her tote bag and placed two of them in a kitchen cupboard. She opened the other and prepared a bottle for her son. After he finished the bottle, she carried him upstairs and tucked him into the cradle. Jessica changed into a long nightshirt and lay down on her old bed. She was asleep in a matter of seconds.

The smell of bacon and coffee greeted Jessica the next morning as she slowly awakened. Her mom had always been an early riser, and the familiar smells took Jessica back to her childhood days. Her son was also awake, and he began to cry softly. Jessica picked him up and unbuttoned her nightshirt so that he could suckle on her breast. Holding her son in her arms, she stood and slowly made her way downstairs to the kitchen. There stood her mom, keeping a watchful eye on the bacon as it fried on the stovetop.

"Good morning, Mom."

Harriet Long turned and looked at her. "Do you think it's proper to breast-feed your son in the kitchen? I know you lack moral decency, but for God's sake, your father might see you."

Jessica had expected this opening barrage and was not shaken by the hostility and contempt in her mother's voice. She countered with a cheerful tone, "Actually, I put some of his formula in the cupboard last night. I'm sure you must have noticed it. I'm weaning him off the breast milk. Sorry if it offends you."

Her mom looked at her with cold, steely eyes. "Don't try to out-bitch me, Jessica! Let's get something straight right now: I don't want you back in my house. You disgraced me and destroyed my social standing in this town. The only reason you are here is because of your father. I love him, and he has begged and begged me to give you a second chance. I will tolerate your presence, but in the end, we both know that you're not going to stay."

Jessica pulled a bottle of orange juice from the fridge. "Oh, Mom! You're so silly! Of course I'm going to stay! Did you really think that I would come back here without a plan? I watched you manipulate people while I was growing up. You were elected as president of the Twig Association and president of the Band Boosters and the PTA. You were always looking to be a status symbol in your tiny, pathetic world. You always got your way, and the entire time, you made people think it was their idea. All I have to do is manipulate Daddy into letting me stay. After all, I learned from the best."

Jessica's mom took a step toward her, pointing with the steel spatula in her right hand. "You ungrateful little bitch! I made you! I pulled strings to get you on the cheerleading squad. I did everything to make you the most popular girl in Sistersville!"

"That was your dream, Mom. I never asked for it. You only wanted me to be popular so that you looked good."

"And you made sure that didn't happen, didn't you? You went and had an affair with a married man. My life was perfect until then."

"Your bacon is burning." Jessica smirked as she turned and walked into the living room.

Jessica's father was sitting on the sofa, reading the morning paper. "Good morning, Daddy!"

"Well, good morning, young lady! Did you sleep well?"

"Oh, Daddy, I slept like a log! It's so wonderful being home."

Jessica walked over and gave her father a hug. "So, how about we go downtown and get some breakfast?"

"I think your mother is making breakfast, Jess."

"Oh, I was just in there talking to her. She burned the bacon. I think you and I need to spend some quality time together anyway. Plus you will get a chance to show off your grandson to all your buddies!"

"Well, okay. Let me get my shoes on, and we'll head downtown to the diner."

Jessica's mom walked into the living room and shot her daughter a hateful look. "John, I'm going back to bed. I have a terrible headache."

Her husband looked up from tying his shoe. "I'm sorry to hear that. You seemed fine earlier."

"Yes, well … the pain just came on suddenly while I was in the kitchen."

CHAPTER THREE

The calls began streaming in at around 6:00 a.m., and there were a lot of them. Multiple car tires had been slashed all over town during the night. Curtis Knight called Sergeant Steven Andrews at home and asked him to assist him. "I've got twenty-two reports so far, and I can't answer them all."

A few minutes later, Andrews called Curtis back. "They got my squad car, too. Both front tires are cut."

Curtis sighed and advised Andrews that he would come and pick him up. *Make that twenty-three so far,* he thought.

After picking Andrews up, Curtis decided that they could split the complaints between them if he drove his personal vehicle. He drove to his house and told Andrews he would be available by walkie-talkie. "Give me a handful of those incident reports from the trunk, Steven. I'll use my personal camera to take pictures." After deciding which calls each of them would respond to, Andrews drove off in the cruiser. Just as Curtis was backing his car out of the garage, Amy pulled into the driveway. He stopped, put the car in park, and got out to greet his wife. "Hey, babe! How was the nightshift?"

"Long! I only had two patients on my wing, and they both slept through the night."

"Except when you woke them up every hour to ask how they were feeling?"

Amy slapped him playfully on the arm. "Oh, you are sooooo funny!"

"Sorry. Listen, I have to run, babe. Someone slashed a bunch of tires all over town last night."

Amy frowned. She was disappointed that she couldn't spend a few minutes with him. "Okay. Love you!"

She watched him drive off before putting her car inside the garage. She unlocked the kitchen door adjoining the garage, closing and locking it behind her before dropping her keys on the table. As she debated whether to take a shower or soak in a bubble bath before going to bed, the front doorbell chimed. "Oh bother!" she muttered. She walked into the living room and peeked out the window. She saw her friend Marcie Johnson standing on the front porch.

She opened the door and invited Marcie inside. "What are you doing up so early?"

"Curtis called Steven out to help him take reports. Someone slashed a bunch of tires last night, including two on Andrew's police car."

"Yeah, I saw Curtis a few minutes ago when I got home. People are so stupid! What's the point of slashing tires?"

"I know, right? Anyhow, I figured that since I was up, I'd walk over here and see how you were doing. Did you have a good night at the hospital?"

"It was a good night but a long one. I didn't really do much."

"Would you like to go out for some breakfast? We can walk over to the diner if you want. I'm buying!"

Amy was about to say no, but the hopeful smile on her friend's face made her change her mind. "Okay, but give me time to take a quick shower. There's instant coffee in the cupboard over the stove if you want some."

Curtis pulled in front of the newly opened Sistersville Museum at the corner of Diamond and Wells Streets and climbed out of his car. There were two cars parked nearby with slashed tires. The owners were not around, but Curtis began writing up the reports anyway. He jotted down the vehicle identification and license plate numbers, and he took some pictures with his digital camera. He left notes on both windshields, asking the owners to call him with their insurance information and advising them that a report would be on file at the police station the next day.

The next stop was on North Main Street, directly across the street from Sky Williams' house, where Curtis had been the day before. This time, the complainant was waiting for him. Curtis felt a knot forming in his stomach when he saw the car owner, Councilman Bradly Ford.

"Well, it's about time you got here, Knight, considering I called twenty minutes ago and the police station is only half a block away!"

"I apologize, Mr. Ford. I'm a little overwhelmed this morning with the number of complaints. Do you have your vehicle registration handy?"

Ford handed him the registration and insurance cards. Curtis wrote the information down on an incident report and took some pictures of the slashed tires. "I'll have a report typed up by tomorrow. In the meantime, you can contact your insurance company."

"So that's it? That's all you're going to do?"

"At this time, there isn't much else I can do, Mr. Ford. I have many more calls to answer. If anything comes up, you'll be notified."

"Unbelievable! Someone slashes my tires, and you're just going to make a report and leave?"

"Well, unless you know who did it, what else do you expect me to do?"

"The law enforcement in this town is terrible! What were you all doing last night while this was happening? Eating doughnuts at the Par Mar?

"No, sir. I was home sleeping. Have a blessed day."

Curtis drove away and felt his blood pressure rising. He stopped and took one of his pills before continuing on to his next call. While he doubted anyone else was going to get under his skin the way Bradly Ford had, the blood pressure medication was needed anyway. Doc Gwynn would scold him something terrible if he knew Curtis wasn't taking it regularly.

Sergeant Andrews radioed Curtis an hour later, saying he had found something of interest. Curtis drove to his location, and Andrews handed him a baggie that contained a broken plastic box cutter. "I found this under one of the cars, and there's another one just like it across the street by the Chevrolet dealership."

Curtis walked across the street and carefully picked up the second box cutter, dropping it into a clear baggie. "Could we be this lucky, Steven?"

Andrews laughed and replied, "Well, it was a stupid crime, so let's hope the suspect was stupid enough to leave his prints on them!"

"I'm going to take these down to the police station and dust them for prints. Can you handle the rest of these complaints yourself?"

"Sure. There are only six left. No problem."

Curtis drove to the police station and carried the two baggies inside. He slowly and carefully processed them for fingerprints and was pleased to see that he had two perfect partial prints on the second box cutter. *Now I just need a suspect to match them to.*

He placed the box cutters inside an evidence bag, sealed it, and put it inside the evidence locker. He decided to walk over to the hardware store. He knew the owner did inventory every Sunday morning. He walked up to the storefront and tapped on the glass of the display window. The owner, Andy, pulled out some keys and opened the front door. "I hate to bother you on a Sunday morning, Andy. But have you sold any box cutters lately? Like the cheap plastic kind?"

"Well, let's see. I do recall selling a few to Bentley Ford a few days ago."

"Bentley Ford? You mean Bradly's boy?"

"Yes … day before yesterday."

"I see. And would you still have the security camera footage from two days ago?"

"Sure do. I only change it on Monday mornings."

Curtis smiled. "Andy, do me a favor and save that footage for me. I might need it later. I owe you one!"

CHAPTER FOUR

S ky Williams rolled out of bed at around 10:00 a.m. Although he had intended to sleep long into the afternoon, the diary had other plans. He slowly descended the stairs and entered his den. The diary, which sat on top of his writing desk, was glowing orange. Sky eased his slightly overweight body into the chair in front of the desk. At 6′ 1″ he had been a fairly decent athlete in high school. But the years of excessive drinking and junk food were beginning to show. He placed his right hand on the small key, and turned it slowly. A bright orange glow filled the entire room as Sky fell into a deep trance. He sat up straight and rigid in the chair as his left hand picked up a pen and began writing on a tablet at an incredibly rapid rate. His right hand moved only when it flipped a page on the writing tablet. He wrote and wrote for several hours. His eyes were glazed and fixed.

Just as suddenly as it had started, the writing stopped. The orange glow faded back into the book, and Sky's right hand slowly turned the key back to its original position. He then flexed his left hand, rubbing his numb fingers. His eyes began to refocus, and he picked up the writing tablet to read the words he had furiously written for the past two hours. A smile formed on his lips. Soon, he would have another best seller.

Sky had found the diary while doing research in Tennessee two summers ago. He had been attempting to locate the personal diary of Julia Graham, a Sistersville native who had died mysteriously in Hollywood back in 1935. Her story had always fascinated him growing up, and he had been hoping to write an article about her life, but the facts surrounding her death had been hard to come by.

Julia graduated from Sistersville High School in 1933. By all accounts, she was an extremely talented singer and dancer. She was also quite beautiful, and her family was well respected. One day, after withdrawing her life savings from the bank, Julia left town, telling her parents she was going to visit relatives in New York. Instead, she took a bus to Hollywood, where she quickly discovered that the glamourous life she had read about in magazines didn't exist. Work was hard to find. As talented and beautiful as she was, there were hundreds of other girls there who fit that description, too.

She became depressed and attempted suicide by ingesting poison. This actually brought her publicity, and she received a small role in a movie. However, things didn't improve, and she became desperate. She sought the company of a seedy, overweight camera man … who was married. He worked on many films and no doubt promised Julia that he'd help her to land future roles. The two took an overnight trip together while his wife was out of town. When they returned to his home the next night, Julia supposedly shot herself in the head. She died later at the hospital. It was ruled a suicide, but many of the people who knew her best doubted that story. Many secretly believed that the camera man shot her when she threatened to reveal the affair to his wife.

Julia's body was returned to Sistersville. Her family hoped to avoid any publicity, so a secret funeral was held at dawn at her grandmother's home on Main Street, and then her body was taken to Greenwood Cemetery.

Sky had been searching for Julia's personal diary, which had been sent back to Sistersville to her family following her death. The family had since moved away, and his attempts to locate the diary had taken him to several states. So there he was, following up on another lead, in a dilapidated antique store outside of Knoxville. The owner was an elderly African-American woman who wore a long gray dress and a black scarf on her head. Sky introduced himself and told her what he was looking for.

"You have traveled a long way for this diary. But I do not have it. However, I can help you in other ways."

She walked over to a shelf lined with books and pulled one out. "Please have a seat, Mr. Williams."

She placed the book on the table in front of him. He could see that it was a weathered old diary with a key protruding from its metal lock. "Place your hand on top."

He did done so, feeling a little uneasy. But her voice was soothing and gentle.

"Now close your eyes and think of the one you seek. Concentrate and try to picture her face."

The woman then turned the key in the lock, and a bright orange light filled the room. A moment later, she turned the key again, and the light disappeared. Sky was ecstatic, stunned, and a bit frightened.

"Did you see her, Mr. Williams? Did you see the one you seek?"

He *had* seen her! For a split second, Sky had been in the same room with Julia Graham. It had felt real, and he did not care how crazy it all seemed. If he could visit her for longer, he would be able to write one hell of an article! "How much do you want for the diary?"

"It comes with a steep price. However, I do not want money."

"Name your price."

"The price is your soul, Mr. Williams. This diary will make you very rich. But in twenty years, you must pay. Those are my terms, and they are not negotiable."

Sky figured the woman to be a whack job, but he played along. "I prefer to do things on my own terms. So what happens if I die before the twenty years are up? What if I get hit by a car or something?"

"Then your price is waived. But I must warn you, this diary is very powerful. The key must always remain in the lock when in use. You must never remove it."

"What happens if it's removed?"

"If you are inside and the key is removed, then inside you shall remain."

"So, how does it work?"

"You must discover that on your own. One final warning, Mr. Williams: do not lose the key. There are no other copies."

It took Sky Williams about three months to figure out how to use the diary. He quickly forgot about Julia Graham, because he could now visit and communicate with any famous deceased person in history. All he needed to do was imagine them ... and turn the key. With this ability, he was able to gain rare and previously unknown insights into the minds of famous people, such as Albert Einstein, Henry Ford, and Mark Twain.

This became the basis for his best seller, and historians were amazed at the detailed accuracy of his writing. Although much of the personal information he wrote about each man was not always verifiable, there was enough truth in his book to cement his credibility. The eccentric desires, fantasies, and habits of these famous men created a huge fan base for his book and made him a wealthy man.

After his initial success, Sky knew that writing another best seller would make him even richer and more famous. He was now focusing on the evil side of mankind. He wanted to delve into the minds of Hitler, Mussolini, and Jeffrey Dahmer, to name a few. But visiting these evil men was slowly affecting his personality. He began to drink heavily and have dark thoughts. His dreams were frequently nightmares.

CHAPTER FIVE

Amy came downstairs after her shower and found Marcie sitting at the kitchen table, staring into her coffee cup.

"I'll give you a penny for your thoughts."

"Oh, geez! You startled me!" Marcie said as some of her coffee spilled onto the table.

"It's okay, I've got it." Amy walked over to the sink and grabbed a paper towel. She began wiping up the coffee, looking at Marcie with concern. "What's got you so deep in thought?"

Marcie sighed and then slowly looked up at Amy with misty eyes. "What's it feel like to … to … be pregnant?"

Marcie then began to cry, her hands covering her eyes as the tears started to flow heavily.

Amy was caught off guard by this sudden outburst of emotion. "Hey, hey, come on," she said in a soothing voice as she placed her arms around Marcie's shoulders. "Where did all this come from? What's going on?"

After a minute, Marcie calmed down enough to talk. "After you and Curtis found out you were pregnant last month, Steven got all excited. It's all he's talked about lately … having a baby."

"So? That's no reason to be so upset, is it?"

"Amy, I can't have babies. It's medically impossible. I've been to every specialist in the Ohio Valley, and they all say the same thing."

"Oh, Marcie, I had no idea! I'm so very sorry, hon!" Amy hugged her friend tightly as she again began to cry. "Calm down and talk to me, Marcie. I'm here for you."

"Steven doesn't know this yet. I … I haven't told him. I'm scared that when I do, he's going to dump me!"

"Steven wouldn't do that, Marcie. You need to tell him, and the sooner, the better."

Marcie gave Amy an anxious glance. "Tell him? After the way he's gone on and on about having a baby together? And the whole time, I'm agreeing that it would be great! He's going to be pissed!"

"It's not going to be easy, Marcie, but the longer you let this linger, the worse it's going to get. Certainly, you must know that deep down in your heart."

"Every man wants a child, Amy. Why would he stay with me if I can't give him one?"

"You have a lot to learn about men, Marcie. Of course he *thinks* he wants a baby right now. That's because he sees how happy it makes Curtis, and he wants that happiness, too. But if Curtis was happy because he just got a new motorcycle, then Steven would want one of those, too!"

Marcie managed a small smile. "Okay, I see what you're saying. Maybe I will talk to him today. I'm scared, though. I truly love that man."

"I think he loves you, too. A real man will accept more than you can imagine, Marcie. This is not your fault. It's something you have no control over."

"You're right. But I feel like I've been lying to him by hiding the truth."

"Tell him that. Tell him everything you just told me, and I think everything will work out just fine."

Marcie stood and gave Amy a long hug. "I feel much better now. Thank you for being such a great friend."

"So, are we still going to the diner, or what?"

"I'm really not that hungry, Amy. To be honest, I came here this morning with the intention of talking with you about this. I never really wanted to go out. Can you forgive me?"

Now, it was Amy's turn to laugh. "Girl, I have to confess, too. I did *not* want to go to the diner either! All I want to do is curl up in my bed and sleep!"

"Are you still having morning sickness?"

"No, thank the Lord! I did get a little sick a few days ago, but I blamed that on the meatloaf Curtis tried to make me."

"He actually cooked?"

"He *tried* to cook, Marcie. It was a major fail."

Marcie giggled. "I'm glad you didn't invite us over for dinner that day!" She continued, "I think I'll go home and lie down myself. Crying always makes me want to take a nap."

"The truth is always the best way to go, Marcie. If you need to talk again, stop on by. But try to wait at least eight hours from now, okay?"

"Okay, I promise!"

The two friends hugged, and Marcie left. Amy went upstairs, took off her clothes, and lay down on the bed. She reached over and flipped the control knob on the box fan beside the bed to HIGH. She thought about her friend and felt a deep sadness inside. She couldn't imagine how it would feel to be in Marcie's shoes. She slowly ran her hands over her stomach, thinking about the tiny person who was growing inside her. Within a few minutes, she was asleep.

At that very moment, Jessica Long and her father were pushing a baby stroller past Amy's house, stopping across the street to speak to one of the neighbors. Jessica glanced over at Amy's house. It was not a coincidence that she had chosen to walk down this street.

CHAPTER SIX

News of Jessica Long's return was trending in Tyler County. She and her father were pushing her son's baby stroller up and down the sidewalks, going from street to street, and greeting the early risers on this bright Sunday morning. The church services would not begin for another hour, and the older folks were out walking their dogs and going out for breakfast. It took only a single tweet for the avalanche to begin on social media. By the time Jessica had reached the diner on Wells Street, news of her return to the Ville had spread faster than a California wildfire.

While some of the customers greeted her with a smile, most turned away and ignored her. The hushed and excited whispers buzzed from booth to booth loudly enough to be heard but too low to be understood. Jessica realized what was going on. She had planned this day for quite some time. She was here to plant her seeds of revenge, and the soil before her looked promising.

Nancy Grady was the first person to approach them after they were seated. "My! Isn't he a fine-looking young man!" she cooed as she bent over the baby stroller. Jessica picked up a menu and waited. *Here it comes,* she thought. *Just wait for it.*

"What's his name?"

A smile formed on Jessica's lips. She had reeled in the first fish of the day. "I just call him Junior right now. We aren't sure if he will take his father's first name yet."

Nancy frowned. It was slight, but Jessica noticed it.

"Well, he certainly is a handsome little fellow," Nancy said.

"Why, thank you! He takes after his dad, don't you think?"

The obvious confusion on Nancy Grady's face almost caused Jessica to laugh out loud. Nancy smiled a little awkwardly and left without further comment. Jessica watched Nancy take a seat a few booths away, and she saw her pull her cell phone out of her purse. *Too easy,* Jessica thought.

After the waitress took their order, Bradly Ford walked over to their booth. "Good morning, John. It's nice to see you again, Jessica. You look as pretty

Steven E. Winters

as your mother! The apple doesn't fall far from the tree."

"Well, let's hope this apple ages better when it ripens," she replied with a hint of sarcasm.

Bradly didn't seem to notice, and he bent over to get a closer look at her son. "Now that is a good-looking kid!"

"Yes. I think he looks just like his dad, don't you?"

Bradly gave her a curious look and said, "You folks enjoy your meal. Hope to see you in church later."

"Thank you, Mr. Ford. You have a great day."

Jessica was ecstatic. She couldn't have chosen two people more capable of spreading rumors than the two she had just spoken to. No one else came over to their table after that. Their meals arrived, and Jessica dove into hers. She was starving, and the bacon and eggs were cooked to perfection. Her father, however, seemed withdrawn and troubled, but that didn't upset her. Still, it needed to be addressed. He was an important part of her plan. She needed him as a buffer between her and her mother until she exacted her revenge on this town. "What's wrong, Daddy? You've hardly touched your breakfast. Are you feeling okay?"

"I don't know, Jess. Before we left the house this morning, I spoke to your mother. She seems to think that your being here is bad for us."

"Did she mean bad for you both or bad for her?"

"Please don't put me in the middle again, Jess. You know how I feel about you. It broke my heart when you left and moved to South Carolina."

"I had to, Daddy. Mom was becoming impossible to live with. I made a mistake, okay? But having an affair with a married man wasn't the worst thing I could have done as a teenager. I never did drugs, never smoked, never drank alcohol; yet, the one mistake I made sent her into crazy lady land!"

"Jess, it wasn't just about you and Curtis Knight. Your mother tried to make peace with that. She figured that in a few months, it would pass over like a summer storm and be forgotten."

"She was worried about her own reputation, not mine. Why did she go after Curtis like she did? I mean, if she was really trying to forget about it, then why did she file a complaint with the city? Why did she hire a lawyer and try to sue him? I'd hardly call that making peace!"

Her father slammed his fist on the table, startling Jessica and attracting the attention of the diner's remaining breakfast crowd. "It was because of the others, Jess! If you had just stopped with Curtis, things would have been okay. We might still be a family. But you had to rebel and sleep with other men after your affair with him. *That* is why your mother went after Curtis. She was trying to deflect attention from the men you were sleeping with after him. She thought that if the affair with Curtis was kept alive in the public eye, then what you were doing with those other men would go unnoticed."

Jessica was speechless. How did her parents know about the other men? The answer came to her almost immediately. She lived in a small town! Word got around, and in an ironic twist, she was using that same method today to spread her own rumors. This outburst from her father was an unexpected glitch in her plans, but she recovered quickly.

"Oh, Daddy, I am so sorry!" she wailed as the tears began to stream down her face. "I never ever meant to hurt you! After Curtis, I was torn up inside. I really thought he loved me. Those other guys came around and told me that they weren't like him. They said they really cared about me. I was just looking for love, Daddy!"

As she buried her face in her hands, Jessica hoped that this little ploy was convincing enough. A moment later, she felt his hands on her shoulders. "I'm sorry, Jess. I know you didn't do those things to hurt me. It's just hard for a father to hear those kinds of rumors about his little girl. I would get so angry. You must have felt so alone back then."

"I love you, Daddy. I'm not alone anymore. I'm home."

Her father stood and went to the cashier to pay the bill. Jessica removed her hands from her face. The tears had been shut off. She turned on her cell phone and scrolled to her Facebook account. A sly smile slowly played across her lips. Things were going very well.

When her father returned to the booth, Jessica told him he should head home without her. "I know you're tired, Daddy, and I have so many friends to visit. I'll be home in a few hours."

CHAPTER SEVEN

Officer Rob Hyatt pecked away at the typewriter, finishing up the last of the incident reports from the slashed-tire cases. Chief Knight had asked him to come in a few hours before his afternoon shift began to help him get the reports completed. "You know, Chief, it would be a lot easier if we just used a computer."

Curtis chuckled. "I've heard that song before, Rob. Steven Andrews used to sing it every day from the very same chair you're sitting in."

"I'm just saying it would be more efficient, that's all."

"You mean easier, and yes, it would be. But until the city can budget a few computers for us, we'll have to do it the old-fashioned way."

"Okay, Chief. I don't really mind, seeing as I'm getting some extra hours out of it."

"Speaking of which, I do believe I'll give you the keys and get out of here. Sundays are usually slow, so you shouldn't have any problems. If you need me, call my cell."

Curtis tossed the rookie cop his keys and glanced at the clock on the wall. It was noon, and Amy would be fast asleep. With no other plans for the afternoon, he decided to walk over and visit his old friend Sky Williams.

Sky was picking up the Sunday paper from his front porch when Curtis saw him. "Up early, I see!"

Sky looked up at the sun and shaded his eyes with his hand. "It burns! It burns! What is this wicked orb in the sky that glows so fiercely?"

Curtis laughed as he climbed the stairs onto the front porch. "Save that one for your next book! I'm shocked to see you up this early on a Sunday. I usually see your paper lying on the sidewalk all day."

"A man has to earn a living, Curtis. You never know when the passion to write will strike."

"Working on another book already? I figured you would bask in your limelight for a few months. What's the rush?"

"When the iron's hot, you use it. Besides, if I wait too long, some young buck will write a better book, and Hollywood will forget me."

The two men entered the living room, and Curtis plopped down on the sofa. He picked up Sky's novel and flipped through it. "You know,

Sky, you were always a good writer. But this … this is incredible stuff. How on earth did you find all this personal information about these people?"

"I asked them," Sky replied.

Curtis started to laugh again but noticed that Sky was not smiling. "What do you mean?"

"I meant just what I said. I asked them."

Curtis studied his friend's face, waiting for him to smile. But Sky stared back at him with a solemn expression. "Is this the part where you yell 'Gotcha!' and start to laugh? Because all the people you wrote about are long dead."

Sky sat down on the recliner directly across from Curtis. "I am not joking. Do you have to be anywhere soon? I can tell you the whole story, but it will take time."

For the next fifteen minutes, Sky related the story of how he came to find the mysterious diary in the mountains of Tennessee and about the incredible powers it held.

"So what you're telling me is that you can visit any person in history simply by thinking about them?"

"Yes. I think about them, and then I turn the key. There's a rush of cold air, and I feel like I'm being pulled through a bright tunnel of orange light. Then I'm there … with that person. I can talk to them, Curtis! Face to face with any famous person in history! Can you imagine?"

"This is a great prank, Sky. Really, it's one of your best. But come on ..."

"Listen to me, Curtis! How do you think I found out all that personal information about those people? How could I possibly know that Albert Einstein couldn't button his own shirt or tie his own shoes? How could I know that Mark Twain heard voices in his head when he wrote? They told me! Think about it! How did I go from being a mediocre writer to a famous one in a matter of months?"

"You could have made most of it up. Who could argue with your facts when the people you wrote about are long dead?"

"But a lot of my facts *were* verified, Curtis! Historians acknowledged most of my findings as being true. You know that."

"So you're telling me that this diary takes you to the person you want to talk to. How do you get back?"

"I never leave … not physically, anyway. My body stays behind."

"No, I meant how do *you* get back … the part of you that's inside the diary?"

"When I have enough information for the day, I simply think about being back in my body. That's it. I wake up."

"That's quite a story, Sky. It just seems a little too farfetched for me to believe."

"Come on, Curtis! After all the stories I've heard about you and ghosts? I thought that of all the people I know, you would be most receptive to this. I'm disappointed in you. But they say that the proof is in the pudding, so come on. I want to show you the diary."

They walked into the den, and Sky asked Curtis to have a seat at the desk. "Now, put your hand on top of the diary, think of someone you want to talk to who is dead, and then turn the key. Since you haven't used the diary before, I'll be here to bring you back."

"Why can't I bring myself back?"

"It's very difficult to do. It took me nearly three months to learn how to get back when I wanted to. Sometimes, I'd be in there for hours. The concentration has to be intense. Don't worry! I'll bring you back in a few seconds."

Curtis placed his hand on the diary and closed his eyes. After a few seconds, he turned the key. The room filled with bright orange light, and Curtis's body suddenly became stiff and still. After ten seconds had elapsed, Sky reached down and turned the key back.

Curtis slowly opened his eyes, blinked several times, and then looked up at Sky. A huge grin crossed his face. "Holy shit! I just saw Marilyn Monroe!"

CHAPTER EIGHT

T he sound of the front door opening startled
Marcie, causing her to drop the paring knife
she was using to slice a cucumber over the kitchen
sink. "You scared me, Steven! I didn't hear you
pull up."

"Sorry about that! I had to drop Curtis's cruiser
off at the police station, so I walked home. The city
crew will be here later to replace the tires on my
cruiser. What are you making over there?"

"Mrs. Robinson stopped by an hour ago with
some fresh tomatoes and cucumbers from her
garden, so I thought I'd make us a salad for lunch."

"That sounds great! But I'm really craving
something a little more substantial than salad.
Why don't we walk up to the Wells Inn and eat? I
hear they're serving roast beef today. We can have
the salad tonight."

"Okay. Did you get all of your reports finished?"

"Yes, and I turned them all over to Rob Hyatt.
It's really nice having someone else to do the
typing now," he said with a laugh.

Marcie finished making the salad while Steven washed up. She covered the bowl with some plastic wrap, placed it in the fridge, and walked over to the sofa. She sat down and waited for Steven to come into the living room. He walked in and began looking around. "Have you seen my wallet?"

"Steven, I need to talk to you. It's very important. Please sit here with me."

"What's wrong, Marcie?"

She took a deep breath after he sat next to her. She took his hand in hers and looked into his eyes. "I love you with all my heart and soul, Steven. There is something about me you need to know."

Marcie felt his hand tighten in hers as she began to talk. She told him about the multiple doctor visits and tests she'd had over the years and how the experts had all arrived at the same diagnosis. "Steven, I can't have kids."

Steven stared at the floor. A full minute went by as he processed what Marcie had told him, and then he spoke, "Why are you telling me this now?"

"Because you've been talking nonstop about how cool it would be to have a baby since you found out about Amy being pregnant."

"And you didn't say a word. You just let me go on and on, knowing all along that it was something you could never do for me." He stood up and walked across the room. He stood with his back to her for a moment and then turned to face her. "I'm really pissed off at you!"

Marcie bowed her head and waited for the end to come. She was prepared for it. She expected it. He was going to dump her. "I know you must hate me, Steven. I'm sorry. I knew that if I told you I couldn't have your child, you'd break up with me. That's why I didn't tell you before. I was scared to!"

"I'm not mad because you can't have my child, Marcie. I'm mad because you didn't have enough faith and trust in me to tell me in the first place. That's deception, and it's just as bad as lying."

"Please don't leave me, Steven! I couldn't live without you! You're all I have in this world."

"I'm going for a walk."

Marcie curled up on the sofa after he stormed out the front door. Her fears were coming true.

Steven began walking toward the city park. His mind was in a fog. What Marcie had said about not being able to have kids was a tremendous shock to him. The fact that she had not told him sooner was even worse. He could learn to accept their being a childless couple, but the part about her lying hit him in the gut … hard.

Jessica Long was sitting on a bench by the walking trail along the river when she saw Steven Andrews heading toward the park shelter. She stood and quickly pushed the stroller out of the park. She walked the short distance to his house and pulled a manila envelope from the pouch at the back of the stroller. She placed it inside the mailbox on his front porch, rang the doorbell, and then hurried off. She returned to the park, where she found Steven sitting at a picnic table beneath the shelter. "Hello, stranger!"

Steven looked up and his eyes grew wide. "Jessica! What the ….? When did you get back in town?"

"You don't seem very happy to see me!"

"Why should I be? You caused a lot of damage in this town. Why are you back?"

Jessica pointed at the stroller. "I wanted my son to meet his father. Why don't you pick up your son and say hello?"

"What? What in the hell do you mean … *my son*?"

"Oh don't act so surprised, Steven! We did have sex, you know! Do I need to tell you the story about the birds and the bees?"

"You slept with a lot of guys before you left town. What makes you so sure that I'm the father?"

"Because, silly, after Curtis dumped me and I slept with those other men, I got my period. You were the last one I slept with after that."

"We had sex *one time*, Jessica! Do you honestly think you're going to pin this on me?"

"I thought you would be much happier than this to meet your son! I'm disappointed in your reaction."

"You'll need to prove it! Now get out of my sight!"

"Tsk, tsk. I pray that your son doesn't inherit that temper of yours! As for proving it, I intend to do just that. I dropped off the DNA test paperwork at your house along with a copy of the birth certificate."

"You did *what*? When?"

"Just a few minutes ago."

"Oh God, no! Marcie!" Steven stood up and took off running.

Marcie wiped the tears from her eyes and got up to answer the door. No one was there, but a manila envelope was poking out of the mailbox. She walked into the kitchen and opened it. She pulled out the birth certificate and felt the room begin to spin as she read the words:

CHILD'S FULL NAME: Steven Michael Andrews, Jr.

MOTHER'S FULL NAME: Jessica Lynn Long

FATHER'S FULL NAME: Steven Michael Andrews

A switch flipped somewhere deep inside Marcie's mind. She laid the certificate on the table and walked over to the kitchen sink. She reached down, picked up the paring knife, and studied the serrated edge of the blade.

CHAPTER NINE

After Steven Andrews left, Jessica took a seat at the picnic table, pulled her son from his stroller, and pulled out one of the bottles of formula she had packed in the diaper bag. She slowly rocked him back and forth and hummed a song as he eagerly sucked on the nipple. He was a well-behaved baby who hardly ever cried. She was thankful for that. After he finished, she burped him and changed his diaper. "Okay, Junior! Let's see how much more damage Mommy can do today."

It was getting close to 3:00 p.m., and Jessica was beginning to tire. She was walking on Main Street and was about to turn up Diamond Street to head for home when she spotted Bradly Ford on his front porch. She pushed the stroller up the street and shouted out to him, "Hey, Bradly!"

He looked at her and then scanned the street to see if anyone was watching. "What do you want, Jessica?"

"Calm down, dude! I just wanted to let you know that you're not the father. I knew you were worried. I could tell by how closely you were checking my son out at the diner."

"Well, umm … yes, I was a little curious. It wouldn't be good for me or my political career to be the father. I'm sure you understand."

"Of course I do! Remember who my mother is! I know how important social status is to people like you."

"Well, I *was* one of the councilmen who pushed for Curtis Knight to be fired after your affair became public. Imagine what the gossips in this town would do to me if they knew I slept with you, too!"

"You mean the voters, don't you?" she replied with a laugh.

Bradly did not laugh back. "So, whose baby is it? Curtis Knight's?"

"You'll find out soon enough, Bradly. Say, who's the new guy across the street?"

Bradly looked over and replied, "That's Sky Williams, the author."

"Is he a friend of yours?"

"No! That man drinks too much and has women over there all the time. He's a good buddy of Curtis Knight, though."

"Hmm, now that's interesting. Well, nice seeing you, Bradly," she said as she crossed the street.

"Hello, Mr. Williams."

Sky looked up from his Sunday paper and nodded. "Hello there. Do I know you?"

"My name is Jessica Long. I believe we have a mutual friend."

Sky recognized her name. He had heard all about her affair with Curtis Knight when he was living in North Carolina. Facebook made it a small world. "If you're referring to Curtis Knight, then yes, we do," he said with a guarded smile. "As a matter of fact, you just missed him."

"Oh, did I? What a shame. May I come up on the porch? The sun is really hot."

Sky ran his eyes up and down Jessica's body. She was a stunning beauty with long blonde hair and a curvaceous body that fit her short frame perfectly. He could see why Curtis had strayed. "Sure! Come on up! I'll grab us some sweet tea from the kitchen. Have a seat."

She lifted the stroller onto the porch and took a seat on the swing. Junior was sleeping peacefully.

She noticed a book on a table beside her and picked it up. Its title was *Inside the Great Minds of History.* There were several glowing reviews on the front jacket and a picture of Sky Williams on the back. She was impressed. As she flipped through the pages, Sky returned with the tea.

"So, you're a big-time writer, huh? I've never met one before."

He blushed slightly. "Not big-time … not yet. I'm working on my next book right now. Hopefully, it will be better than the first."

"What if it's not? I mean, if you write a classic like *Gone with the Wind* or *The Grapes of Wrath,* do people even care if you write anything else?"

"My book is not *that* good. I'm hoping to be remembered for more than one book. Do you read a lot?"

"Not anymore. I did when I was younger, though. A good book will take you places, you know? It will make you feel like you are right there."

"Yes, I do know. I know only too well."

"May I use your bathroom Mr. Williams?"

"Of course, and you can call me, Sky. Come on in. It's too hot to sit out here in the heat, especially for a baby."

"That is very sweet and kind of you, Sky. Most men aren't that caring when it comes to little ones," Jessica said gratefully.

Once inside the house, Sky showed her where the bathroom was. When she had finished, he asked her if she would like something a little stronger to drink. "I can't, Sky. I still breast-feed Junior sometimes, so I don't put alcohol or drugs in my body. But you can drink if you like. I don't mind. Besides, it feels so nice and comfortable in here. I'd love to hear about your life while I cool off. It must be fascinating being a famous writer!"

For the next hour and a half, Sky drank and talked about his life growing up and his book. After he had polished off his fourth vodka and tonic, Jessica asked him, "So, where did the inspiration for your novel come from?"

Sky was feeling a little buzzed, and Jessica was looking sexier by the minute. He was beginning to think he might have a shot at sleeping with her. Despite the fact that he knew she was trouble, Sky didn't care. He seemed to be drawn to bad women lately … like the Harris twins. He stood up and made himself another drink. Jessica noticed that he was slurring his words slightly. She began to consider having sex with him. Although he wasn't exactly attractive and was overweight, he was rich. Rich men could be manipulated just as easily as poor men could, and if she ever needed money, he would likely pay up.

"So you really want to know where I got my inspiration from? Well, I'll tell you … it came from the mouths of the people I wrote about! They told me!"

Jessica knew that he was drunk now, but she was curious to find out what he was talking about. She slid over on the sofa until her leg touched his. She leaned against him, placing her head on his shoulder. She looked up into his eyes. "You're a remarkable man, Sky."

He leaned over and kissed her. As his hands began pawing at her clothes, she felt the smugness growing inside her. Like any woman who had ever felt betrayed by a man, the incredible self-satisfaction that could be gained by sleeping with one of his best friends had nothing to do with physical pleasure. It was pure revenge.

CHAPTER TEN

I t was well past 7:00 p.m. when Jessica Long pushed her stroller up the steep grade of Prospect Street onto McCoy Heights. She had loved running up and down the many steps that led from Diamond Street to the Heights as a youngster, but climbing them with a stroller in tow was out of the question. She was physically exhausted, and her son was crying. All she wanted to do was get to her parents' house on Washington Street and take a shower. The day had been long but very rewarding. In fact, the visit with Sky Williams had added a new twist to her plans. She lifted her son from his stroller and carried him into the house. Her father was stretched out on the sofa watching 60 *Minutes*, and her mother was in the sewing room. Jessica knew that the sewing room was actually her mother's drinking room.

Jessica went into the kitchen, opened the fridge, removed a bottle of formula, and popped it into the microwave. She rocked her little boy as she waited, whispering into his ear as his cries slowly became whimpers. After testing the formula on her wrist, she placed the nipple in her son's mouth. While he ate, she carried him into the living room. "Daddy, would you mind feeding Junior while I take a shower?"

"Where have you been, Jess? I was getting worried."

"I ran into some old friends. Time just flew by."

He sat up and took the baby in his arms. Jessica gave her father a quick kiss on the forehead and headed upstairs. She carefully removed an object from her pocket and laid it under the pillow on her bed before going into the bathroom. She removed her clothes and stood under the scalding water of the shower, washing away the less-than-pleasant memory of sleeping with Sky Williams just one hour before.

After toweling off, Jessica lay on top of her bed naked. She stretched, taking note of the tan lines on her legs and arms. She got up, opened a suitcase, removed a white silk bathrobe, and slipped it on. She then reached under her pillow and pulled out the object she had stolen from Sky's house. She studied it for a few moments, considered her options, and decided to put her new plan into action.

She stood and walked downstairs to the living room, where her father was stretched out on the sofa snoring, and her son was fast asleep on his chest. Rather than taking in the moment and enjoying this precious bond between grandfather and grandson, she was relieved that they were both asleep and out of her way. She walked over to her mother's sewing room and knocked lightly on the door.

"Yes?"

"Mom, it's me. I want to talk to you. Daddy and Junior are asleep on the couch. Can you please listen to me for a few minutes without yelling?"

There was no reply. Jessica opened the door and saw her mother sitting in a rocking chair, staring at the floor. "Mom, did you hear me?"

Her mother looked up at her with glassy eyes and nodded. "Go ahead and talk," she said in a slurred voice.

"I've been doing a lot of thinking since I got home last night, Mom. You were right about me all along. I never did appreciate all the things you did for me when I was a child. I guess it took me having a child of my own to understand the sacrifices you have to make as a parent. I lost my freedom when Junior was born. Now when I make plans for the day, they must include him. I'm not independent anymore."

Her mom took a drink from the wine glass in her hand. "You don't know the half of it, Jessica. Being a mom means doing the best for your kid even when it means losing what you have or want."

"I understand that now. Being in town today took me back. I remembered being a carefree teenager, and now I realize that the reason I enjoyed that time in my life was because you made it all possible."

"You're damn right! I gave up a lot for you. My mom did the same thing for me."

Jessica seized upon the reference to her grandmother and continued, "Of course she did. Grandma was a wonderful woman. I miss her so much. I bet you do, too."

Her mom lowered her eyes and whispered, "I miss her every day."

"That's why I was so surprised when I found Grandma's diary in my room tonight! I was dragging my suitcase out of the closet, and a floorboard came loose. I pulled it up, looked inside, and there it was. She must have hidden it in there when she was a child growing up in this house. Isn't that incredible?"

Her mother's eyes grew wide, and her voice rose with excitement. "You found my mom's diary?"

Yep, I sure did! I read some of it, too."

"You … you read it?"

"Why don't you come and see? It's up in my room."

Her mom stumbled slightly as she got out of the rocking chair. Jessica quickly crossed the room and grabbed her arm to steady her. They walked up the steps to Jessica's room, and there on the bed lay the diary. Jessica led her mom over to the bed, and the two of them sat down.

"I want you to close your eyes and think about grandma. Just put your hand on top of the diary and think about your mom. Can you see her in your mind?"

"Yes, I can! Oh, this is so wonderful! I can't wait to read what …"

At that moment, Jessica turned the key on the diary she had stolen from Sky Williams, and an orange glow filled the room. Her mom's eyes became blank, and her body became rigid. She sat on the bed like a statue, her breathing slow and shallow. Jessica reached over and plucked the key from the lock, slipping it inside the pocket of her robe. She pulled and tugged on her mother's limp body until she got her inside the closet. She then took the diary and dropped it into her suitcase. She would figure out what to do with her mother tomorrow. Right now, she just wanted to sleep.

Jessica walked back downstairs and entered the living room. She picked Junior up carefully, not wanting to awaken her father. She took him upstairs, changed his diaper, and tucked him in. She then fell back on the bed and smiled. She had come home with the intention of staying long enough to get revenge on everyone who had shunned her two years ago. Maybe now she would stay for a while. With her mother out of the way, she was now in charge of the house.

CHAPTER ELEVEN

Curtis had rushed home from Sky's house, full of excitement and awe. He could hardly wait to tell Amy about the diary and his experience. Since she wouldn't be up for another thirty minutes, he decided to reheat the chili and make a batch of corn bread. He preheated the oven and began mixing the eggs, milk, and corn bread mix in a bowl. He then used some cooking spray to coat a 9' X 9' glass baking dish. Just as he was about to pour the thick dough into the baking dish, the front doorbell chimed. He put the bowl down and went to answer the door.

Steven Andrews was standing in the doorway when Curtis opened the front door. He looked upset, and Curtis thought he detected some puffiness under his eyes. "What's wrong?"

"I need to talk to you in private. Is Amy awake yet?"

"She should be anytime. Why?"

"Can you come outside, please? I need to tell you something."

Steven's tone of voice was both serious and sad. Curtis stepped out onto the porch, shutting the door behind him. "Okay, what is it?"

"Jessica Long is back in town."

Curtis felt his blood pressure rising, followed by a queasy feeling in the pit of his stomach.

Steven continued, "And that's not all. She's got a little boy with her. She claims he belongs to me."

"You? How is that possible? Steven, please tell me you didn't—"

"I did. But that was before we were friends, Curtis. I was getting ready to leave for the police academy, and you were having all those personal issues with Amy. It was just the one time."

Curtis leaned against the porch railing. A dull, thumping pain was forming in his temples. "You slept with Jessica Long after you saw all the crap she put me through? What were you thinking?"

"I wasn't thinking, Curtis! I was having a few beers at the Elks Club, and she came over and started flirting with me. One thing led to another … and … well …" Steven's voice trailed off as he looked at the ground. "It's nothing I'm proud of."

"Okay. What's done is done. When did she tell you that the little boy was yours?"

"Marcie and I had a fight earlier today, and I walked down to the park to cool off. Next thing I know, Jessica was standing next to me. But that's not the worst part of this, Curtis. She dropped off some DNA test paperwork and a copy of the birth certificate at my house … and Marcie saw them."

Curtis whistled and shook his head. "That must have been a shock for Marcie!"

"It was, considering the fight we had was about her not being able to have kids! Then she finds out I might already have one with another woman."

"Marcie can't have kids? Wow. Steven, I'm sorry. I didn't know."

"I went home and tried to reason with her, but she went a little crazy. At first, she was waving a knife around saying she was going to kill herself. I finally got her calm enough to listen to my side of the story. Her sister is down there with her now."

"You said she left a birth certificate? So I'm guessing she listed you as the biological father?"

"Yes, and it's the real deal. But when I think about it, that kid didn't look anything at all like me."

"Oh? Who did it look like?"

"He looked like you Curtis. He was the spitting image of you."

"Who is the spitting image of Curtis?" Amy said as she opened the door and stepped outside.

Curtis felt the pain in his temples increasing. He wondered how much she had heard. It didn't matter; she was going to find out anyway.

"Steven, tell Amy everything you just told me. I need to go take a pill."

Curtis walked back into the house to take his blood pressure medicine and remembered the corn bread. He picked up the bowl of batter, his hands shaking slightly, and put it in the fridge, then turned off the oven. *Was Jessica's kid his?*

Fifteen minutes later, Amy and Curtis walked with Steven to his house. Marcie ran to Amy's arms as soon as they entered. Her sister gave Steven a dirty look and then left. While Amy consoled Marcie, Curtis picked up the envelope from the kitchen table and examined the contents. "This DNA test might clear you, Steven. You should take it."

"Do you think she would encourage me to if she had any doubts?" Steven replied sullenly.

"I guess you've never played poker. She might be bluffing."

"Well, I need to know one way or the other. I'll do it."

Steven walked into the living room and sat next to Marcie. "Baby, I'm sorry for walking out on you earlier today. It's just that you've never kept anything from me before. I didn't know how to react. I don't want to be with anyone else. What happened between that girl and me was long before you and I met, and it's not going to come between us. I love you, Marcie Johnson."

Marcie buried her head in his shoulder and told him that she loved him too. Amy gave Curtis a knowing look, and the two left quietly.

As they walked home, Amy looked at Curtis and asked, "So what if it is your baby? Steven said it looked just like you. What are you going to do?"

"My … my baby?" he stuttered. "But didn't you hear what Steven said? Jessica told him she had her period after she and I split."

"I'm not sure I can handle this Curtis. The affair was bad enough…but a baby?"

They returned home, and Amy got ready for work. She hardly spoke to him and did not kiss him before she left. Curtis sat in his recliner and fought the urge to throw up. His stomach was roiling and in knots. All the bad memories were slowly creeping back into their lives. Would they be able to withstand it all again?

CHAPTER TWELVE

With his head pounding Sky Williams tried to sit up and balance himself on his bed. He was still drunk, that was for certain. He tried to focus on the red LED display on his bedside alarm clock. After a few seconds, he could see that it read 7:58 p.m. He groaned and finally managed to sit up. He had to pee, but getting to the bathroom might prove too difficult. He briefly considered just peeing on the floor and going back to sleep, but then he thought better of it. After sitting still for a minute, he concluded that he did not have the bed spins, which meant he should be able to traverse the short distance to the bathroom without falling down and splitting his head wide open.

He shuffled slowly across the wooden floor and stood in front of the toilet. After nearly a minute of emptying his bladder, Sky felt a little better. He then realized that he was naked, and the haze slowly cleared from his mind. He remembered Jessica Long being in his bed, and a smile played across his lips. She was, without doubt, the best-looking woman he had ever slept with. Unfortunately for him, the alcohol was depriving him of his memories of the actual deed.

He saw a pair of sweatpants on the floor by the bathtub and slipped them on before slowly descending the stairs, holding on to the bannister until he reached the bottom. He noticed the empty vodka bottle on the coffee table in the living room and felt a sudden urge for a drink. He made his way to the den, where he kept his stash of liquor. As he entered the room, he suddenly froze. The top of his desk was bare, save for a pen and his writing tablet. The diary was gone!

He stumbled over to the desk, sweat pouring from his face. He searched the entire den. Now in a panic, he began ransacking every room in his house. After an hour of searching, he fell to the floor and began to weep. It was gone. A wave of despair washed over him. He was finished as a writer. That's when Jessica Long popped back into his head. *Of course! She must have taken it!* In his drunken attempt to impress her, he had shown her the diary and told her the story of its powers. After they had gone upstairs to his bedroom, he must have passed out. Sky cursed himself and called Curtis Knight.

"Hello?"

"She stole my book, Curtis! It's gone! It had to be her!"

"Sky, is that you? What are you talking about?"

"That girl Jessica Long! She stole my book!"

"I don't understand, Sky. Jessica Long stole your book? You mean your novel?"

"No, you idiot! The other one!"

Curtis was not in the mood to be insulted. "Listen, pal, you need to calm down, because if you call me an idiot one more time, I'm going to come up there and bust you in the mouth!"

"Curtis, she stole the *diary*! Jessica Long stole the diary!"

"Look, let me walk up there, and you can tell me what you're talking about, because you're not making sense right now. Give me five minutes."

Curtis hung up and shook his head. He hadn't heard Jessica's name in two years, and today it seemed to be on everyone's lips. He grabbed his keys and drove the police cruiser up to Sky's house. As he climbed out, Bradly Ford called to him from his front porch, "I hope you're here to arrest that drunk! He's been throwing things and screaming for over an hour now!"

"Actually, I'm here to answer a complaint, Mr. Ford. I have no intention of arresting anyone."

"Well isn't that just typical! I thought you were sworn to serve and protect? Or does that only apply to your buddies and your whores?"

Curtis took a step toward Bradly. "Excuse me? Do you have something on your mind?"

"First, your buddy across the street there has two girls fighting in his front yard. Today, I saw your little jail-bait girlfriend over there, and now he's drunk and disturbing the peace. Gee, what are the odds that you're not going to do anything about it?"

"I have to hear a disturbance to make an arrest, Mr. Ford. Right now, I don't hear anything."

"Of course you don't! You didn't hear anything the night my tires got slashed either now, did you? Maybe you were too busy playing cops and robbers in the back of your squad car with Jessica Long!"

Curtis strode up to Bradly Ford until their faces were just inches apart. "I want you to think very carefully about the next words that come out of your mouth, Bradly," Curtis hissed. "They had better be polite and civil. And just so you know, anything other than 'good night' will not be acceptable." Bradly took a step back, turned around, and walked quickly into his house.

Curtis walked across the street and banged on Sky's door. His friend opened it and led Curtis to his den. "See, it's not there! I've looked everywhere!"

"You said Jessica Long stole it. Did you see her take it? Why was she even here?"

"She just showed up this afternoon. I knew who she was, and she seemed impressed that I was an author. One thing led to another and …"

Curtis groaned. "My God! You mean you slept with her, too? For crying out loud, is there *anyone* in this town who *hasn't* slept with her? Please tell me that you didn't show her how the diary works!"

Sky bowed his head. Curtis sighed. "Okay, so now she has the diary, and she knows how to use it. That's just great!"

"What are we going to do, Curtis?"

"*We* are not doing anything. I'm going home to bed. This is your mess, Sky. I've got my own problems."

CHAPTER THIRTEEN

Curtis was waiting in the kitchen for Amy to arrive home from work. It was 7:15 a.m. He tapped his foot nervously, sipping on a glass of grape juice. He heard her car pull into the garage and walked over to open the door for her. He was apprehensive and scared. How was she going to react to everything that had occurred yesterday? He had slept little, tossing and turning for most of the night. She quickly put his mind at ease by kissing him on the cheek as she walked through the door and giving him a cheerful "Morning, sweetheart!"

She noticed the confused look on his face and laughed. "I'm sorry I left last night without kissing you. The whole Jessica thing just threw me for a loop. I did a lot of thinking at work, and I decided there's no reason to be upset. What's in the past is just that. We'll get through this."

"You don't know how relieved that makes me feel!" Curtis then wrapped his arms around her, holding her so tightly that she finally gasped. "Sweetheart, you're going to squash the baby."

Curtis eased his grip a little but kept her in his embrace.

"I don't feel threatened by her, Curtis. I don't know what kind of game she's playing, but this time, I'm not afraid of losing you."

Curtis told Amy about Sky Williams and the diary, his own personal experience with it, and how he had rushed home to tell her about it before Steven had shown up at their doorstep, causing it to slip his mind. He told her how Jessica had gone to Sky's house and slept with him, apparently stealing the diary while he'd slept.

Amy stared at him, her common sense wanting to doubt every word he had just said. Flashing orange lights and talking dead people? But she knew from their past experiences together that he was speaking the truth. He had never lied to her. "So what are you going to do about the diary? How can you prove she took it?"

"I don't know yet." He glanced at the clock and gave her another big hug. "I've got to get to work, babe. The insurance companies will be calling soon wanting copies of all those tire-slashing reports."

After he had settled in at the office, Curtis made a call to the district attorney and gave him his full report on the tire-slashing cases, including the evidence he had collected and the security footage from the hardware store. The DA instructed him to obtain fingerprints from Bentley Ford as soon as possible. After hanging up, Curtis found the incident report he had taken from Bradly Ford, and he called the cell phone number on it. Reaching the voice mail, Curtis left a message: "Mr. Ford, this is Chief Knight. I am calling you in reference to a lead I have in the tire-slashing case. I need your son to come down to the police station this afternoon at 1:00 p.m. for questioning. I will also need to fingerprint your son. If he does not appear, I will obtain a warrant."

Okay, maybe I enjoyed that a little too much, Curtis thought with a little snicker after he hung up. He justified it by recalling how mean and vicious a person Bradly Ford was. This was a man who had once hired a surveyor and paid him $1,000 just to prove that his neighbor's fence was six inches past his property line. Naturally, he demanded that the fence be moved, and the elderly neighbor had to borrow money from his children to do so. This was also the man who had been good friends with Craig Jones and the man who had stood up in a closed session of the city council a few years ago and demanded that Curtis Knight be fired. His son, Bentley, was still living at home at the age of twenty-three and was seemingly content to remain there until his dad decided to make him leave. Bentley had a mile-long rap sheet of petty thefts and other misdemeanors, and Curtis had recently arrested him for drunk driving.

Only three insurance companies called to request copies of the incident reports. As it turned out, most folks were insured with the same local agencies, so Curtis was able to mail out eighteen of the reports by noon.

He decided to try the new Bon-Bon's diner on South Wells Street for lunch. He drove down and parked by the side of the former NAPA auto parts building. It was a beautiful day, so he had a seat at one of the picnic tables set up on the sidewalk. A young waitress came out and told him the daily specials. He opted for the chicken salad sandwich, potato chips, and sweet tea.

Several cars drove by as he waited for his food, and one of the drivers blew his horn and waved. The waitress returned a few minutes later, and Curtis enjoyed a quiet meal. She returned again in about ten minutes to refill his drink, asking if he cared to try one of their homemade cinnamon rolls for dessert. When she brought it out, Curtis was surprised at how big it was. The heavy coating of sugary-sweet glaze melded perfectly with the warm cinnamon dough. He was considering ordering another one when he noticed the time. He threw a twenty on the table and left. It was nearly 1:00 p.m.

As he pulled in front of the city building, Curtis saw Bradly and Bentley Ford standing outside the entrance to the police station. With them was an older man in a suit, holding a briefcase. It appeared that Bentley had hired an attorney. Curtis walked past the three men and went inside the police station. The three men followed, and Curtis offered them a seat. "Gentlemen, I asked you here because as a result of my investigation yesterday, I've concluded that my main suspect is Bentley Ford. Before we go any further, I am going to show you something." Curtis took out a key, opened the evidence locker, and pulled out the two box cutters. "These were recovered near several cars yesterday. One has partial fingerprints on the handle, which I successfully lifted and stored as evidence. I also spoke to the owner of the local hardware store, who told me that he had sold several of these box cutters to Mr. Bentley Ford on Friday. The owner also has video footage of that purchase being made."

Curtis paused and studied the three men. Bentley was fidgeting and looking at the floor. Bradly was ashen and seemed ill. The attorney met his gaze with a grim smile. Curtis continued, "Now, while I realize that Bentley's purchase of these items could be deemed coincidental and circumstantial, the fact that several of these items were found at two separate crime scenes turns the coincidental knob up a notch to probable. And the law says that when I have probable cause, I can make an arrest. All I need now is to match Bentley's fingerprints with those found on the box cutter."

The attorney cleared his throat and spoke, "May I speak to my client privately, Chief Knight?"

CHAPTER FOURTEEN

Jessica whistled cheerfully as she pulled the light blue pastel sundress from her mother's closet and slipped it on over her head. She had awoken just before noon and was feeling refreshed. She picked Junior up from his cradle, dressed him, and then carried him downstairs to the kitchen. After placing him in a high chair, she pulled a skillet from the dish drainer and placed it on the stovetop. She selected some sausage patties from the fridge and tossed them into the skillet. While they cooked, she placed a bottle of formula in the microwave.

Her father walked into the kitchen as Jessica was removing the sausage from the pan. "Good afternoon, Daddy! How do you want your eggs?"

"Mmm … Smells good, Jess! Over easy, just like always! Where's your mother? She usually makes breakfast."

"She left earlier. She said something about going to visit Grandma."

"She went to the graveyard?"

Jessica shrugged. "I guess. The last time I talked to her, she said she wanted to see her mom. Now, sit down and let me get you some orange juice."

"That sounds great. Boy, my back is stiff as a board! That old couch is better suited to short naps. I can't believe I slept on it all night!"

"I guess we both needed some sleep. Do you want toast? I thought I saw some raspberry jam in the fridge."

"Is … is that one of your mom's dresses?"

"Yes, all my clothes are still in the suitcases and are wrinkled."

"Oh, okay. I thought you would've unpacked by now. Did your mom bring in the newspaper before she left?"

"I don't think so. Do you want me to get it?"

"No, no … that's alright. I'll get it. I need to stretch my back anyway."

He walked outside to the end of the driveway and bent over to pick up the paper. That's when he noticed that his wife's car was still parked in the garage next to his. He went back into the house and walked upstairs to their bedroom. The bed was made, and her keys were lying on the nightstand. Beginning to get concerned, he walked down the hall to Jessica's room and peeked in. He noticed her suitcases were all piled against the wall, except for one, which was next to the closet door. That's when he saw the arm.

Jessica had just cracked an egg into the skillet when she heard the floorboard above her head squeak. In a panic, she turned off the burner and went flying up the stairs to her bedroom. Her father was opening the closet door when she entered the room. "Daddy, don't!"

He turned and looked at Jessica and then turned back to his wife. He felt her pulse, which was very weak. But it was her eyes that sent chills down his spine. They were like blank, empty voids in her face. "Jess, we need to call an ambulance! My God! There's something very, very wrong here! Look at her eyes!"

"No, Daddy, it's okay! She was drinking last night and came in here all confused. She fell into the closet and passed out. I didn't want to worry you, so I let her sleep. She'll be okay!"

Her father stood up and glared at her. "What did you do to her, Jess? Tell me!"

"Nothing, Daddy! I swear! Please! You've got to believe me!"

"No, Jess! Not this time! You did something to her. I've seen her passed out drunk before!" he shouted, turning and pointing at his wife. "This is not drunk! I'm calling an ambulance, and then I'm calling the police!"

"*Please* don't, Daddy! I can explain! Just listen to me!"

"I hate you!" he shouted. "Get out, and don't you ever come back!"

Jessica ran out of the room and down the stairs. Grabbing her keys from the kitchen counter, she ran outside and jumped into her Lexus. With tears streaming down her face, she threw the gearshift in reverse, backed out of the driveway onto Washington Street, and then sped off with her tires screeching against the old, worn bricked street. She realized too late that she was never going to make the sharp left turn onto Prospect Street. She put both feet on the brake pedal and pushed hard, but the car was going too fast. It jumped the curb and plunged down the steep embankment. The front of the Lexus held up well upon impact with the bottom of the hill, its airbag deploying immediately, but Jessica Long was not wearing her seat belt and was ejected through the windshield. She died instantly, her nearly severed head dangling from her neck, held only by a thin strip of skin.

CHAPTER FIFTEEN

T he attorney for Brentley Ford discussed the case with his client before asking Curtis to return to the room. "We have decided to enter a plea of guilty, provided no jail time is imposed. Of course, we will reimburse all the victims and insurance companies involved."

"That's not my call, but I'll be happy to set up a meeting between you and the DA."

The attorney handed Curtis his card and motioned for the other two men to follow him out the door. Curtis slipped the box cutters back into the evidence locker and secured it. That's when he heard the fire whistle going off. A few seconds later, he received a radio call from dispatch: "Signal 6-B, corner of Diamond and Prospect." Curtis rushed out the door to his cruiser. A Signal 6 was an auto accident. A Signal 6-A was an accident with injuries. A Signal 6-B was a fatal accident.

A gruesome scene greeted Curtis when he arrived. The car sat on the sidewalk at the base of the steps to McCoy Heights, its windshield shattered. The front end was smashed, and chunks of dirt and grass were embedded in the grill from its plummet down the hillside. Thick, gray smoke billowed from beneath the crumpled hood, and antifreeze leaked out onto the pavement. About twenty feet away was the driver's body, which someone had mercifully covered with a blanket. Curtis went to the car and checked to see if anyone was inside. He then walked over to the covered body, kneeled down slowly, and lifted the blanket to view the victim. Jessica's lifeless eyes stared back at him. He saw her torn neck, and could literally see down her windpipe. He dropped the blanket and vomited in the street.

The fire trucks arrived just minutes later, followed by the ambulance. While the firemen tended to the car, Curtis looked at the paramedic who came rushing over to him and shook his head sadly. "Her head is cut off. Call the coroner, and ask the funeral director to bring his hearse up here pronto."

The paramedic returned a minute later. "We just got a call to the Long residence up on the heights. Dispatch says the man is hysterical. Is it okay if we clear out from here?"

Curtis nodded. He knew the call had to be linked to the accident. He pulled out his cell phone and called Steven Andrews. "Steven, I need you up here. I've got my hands full."

When Andrews arrived, Curtis briefed him on the body. "We need to get her moved. We'll have a big crowd in a few minutes, and I don't want anyone else to see what I just saw." Curtis went to the trunk of the cruiser and grabbed some chalk that he normally used to mark tires on cars parked in the time-limit zones downtown. He lifted the blanket and slowly drew an outline on the pavement around Jessica's body. He then called the firemen over and asked if they would assist him with moving her body.

"When the hearse arrives, I want to place her body in it quickly. But her head is nearly cut off, and I don't want any onlookers to see that. What I'd like to do is have you fellows lift her body while I hold onto the head. We'll keep the blanket on her. Remember, move slowly!"

A few of the younger firemen looked at each other nervously. They were all volunteers, and some had never seen a dead body. The hearse arrived, and Curtis instructed the funeral director to back up as close as possible to the body. Curtis and the firemen crouched down and lifted the body. He didn't have to see the crowd of onlookers to know that they were all moving closer and straining to catch a peek. He could hear Andrews barking at them to stand back. If they knew what he had seen, they would not have been so anxious. The men lifted the body on the count of three and slid it into the back of the hearse. The funeral director then drove off.

A small pool of blood inside the white chalk marks was all that remained now. To Curtis, it indicated that Jessica must have died instantly. When the heart stops beating, blood stops circulating. Considering the severity of her injury, if she had lived for even a few seconds, there would have been much more blood.

His radio crackled to life as dispatch called him. He was needed at the Long residence, Code 3, which meant *now*. "Steven, can you take over here? Just take photos and measurements for me, okay? Don't let them tow the car until you have everything you need."

Curtis jumped in his cruiser and turned left onto the steep grade of Prospect Street and then right onto Washington Street, pulling in behind the ambulance that was parked in front of the

Long residence. He shut off the ignition and ran into the house.

The paramedic heard him enter and yelled, "Upstairs, Curtis!" He took the steps two at a time. There, sitting on the floor by the closet, was Harriet Long. The EMT was taking her blood pressure. Curtis noticed her eyes right away. "What's going on here?" he panted.

That's when John Long spoke. He was sitting next to some suitcases on the floor. Curtis hadn't noticed him when he'd entered the room. "I don't know what she did to her, but she did something bad! Look at her!"

The paramedic whispered to Curtis, "We found a baby boy crying in the kitchen. My driver is down there with him now. Should we call social services? We really need to transport Mrs. Long to the hospital! Her breathing is shallow, and her heartbeat is dangerously low."

Curtis thought for a minute. "No. You're not going to take her anywhere. There's nothing the doctors can do for her."

The paramedic looked at him with a shocked expression. John Long jumped to his feet and yelled, "What do you mean they're not taking her anywhere? By all that is holy, I'll drive her to the hospital myself if need be! Are you going to try and stop me?"

Curtis remained calm. "Listen, if you will all help me, I can cure her right now."

CHAPTER SIXTEEN

"I need you all to listen to me! There is a small book—a diary—somewhere in this house. I need it. If we can find that diary, I can cure Harriet. I know this sounds crazy, but I want you to look at her eyes. Have you ever seen anything like that before? She's under a spell of sorts, and I can snap her out of it. But I need that diary!"

John Long took a step toward Curtis. "This is nonsense! I'm taking my wife to the hospital right now!"

Curtis unsnapped his holster and pulled out his gun. He held it by the barrel with the grips facing out toward John. "Here. Take it, John. If you think I'm lying, then do what you have to do. But everyone in this room knows I don't lie."

John Long hesitated, his eyes fixed on the gun. A few agonizing seconds passed before he took a step back, his eyes falling to the floor. "Okay, I'll help you look."

The four of them began pulling out drawers and ransacking the closet and bathroom. Finally, the

EMT shouted, "I found it! It was in this suitcase!" He handed the diary to Curtis, who frowned. "The key is missing. We *need* the key! It's a small black key, about an inch long, with a rounded top. Keep looking!"

John Long lifted the mattress from the twin bed and flung it aside. He then lifted the box springs, looked at the carpeting under the bed, and let the springs drop back onto the frame. The paramedic, who was standing behind him, tried to walk around the mattress and tripped. When she fell to the floor, her hand landed on Jessica's robe, and she felt something hard in the pocket. She reached inside and pulled out the key. "I've got it, Curtis!"

"Okay, John put that mattress back, and let's put Harriet onto the bed."

They slowly lifted the unconscious woman onto the bed and laid her down. Curtis placed her hand on top of the diary, placed the key in the lock, and turned it. A bright orange light flowed from the diary, filling the room. Harriet's eyelids fluttered. She suddenly gasped for air and sat straight up. Her eyes opened, and she blinked a few times. She then looked at John and grabbed him, hugging him hard as she began to weep. "Oh, John, it was terrible! I'm so happy to see you, darling!"

John wept a little himself. As tears of relief rolled down face, he said, "Harriet, can you tell me what happened?"

"Well, Jessica told me she had found Momma's diary under a floorboard, and I wanted to read it. I closed my eyes and, suddenly, there I was in a room with Momma ... except it wasn't Momma from when I was a young girl. It was Momma from when I last saw her, right before she died. She had dementia and didn't know who I was! I tried to leave, John, but I couldn't! I was stuck in that room with her, and she kept asking me over and over who I was." Harriet again began to weep.

Curtis motioned for the EMT and paramedic to follow him out into the hallway. "Listen, what you saw in there was just an illusion gone wrong. Jessica hypnotized her mother, and things got crazy. Her mother simply believed it was all real. She'll be fine now."

"What about the baby boy, Curtis?"

"He's Jessica's son. He'll be okay here with his grandparents."

After the ambulance personnel left, Curtis sat at the kitchen table, staring at Junior. "I don't know why Steven said you were the spitting image of me, because you're much more handsome." He picked the boy up and held him. John and Harriet came downstairs into the kitchen. Curtis handed the boy to John. "I need to talk to you both."

After breaking the news of Jessica's death to her parents, Curtis was amazed at the calmness they both displayed. He then broke the news about Steven possibly being the father. "We can raise the boy," John said, "but if Steven is the biological father, then we'll meet with him and see what his wishes are."

Harriet looked at her husband with surprise. "Dear, that's something we need to discuss together. We're rather old to be raising a toddler."

"Would you prefer that we place him in some foster home? He's our blood, Harriet. He's our grandson."

Curtis interrupted them, "I'll notify social services and let them know Junior is here. I doubt if they will object to your caring for him until Steven can take the DNA test. We'll just play it by ear for now."

John followed Curtis outside to his cruiser. "I guess we'll have to make funeral arrangements now. I don't know what happened to her, Curtis.

For the first eighteen years of her life, she was a wonderful daughter. Then it was like the devil got inside her. I never should have let her come home …"

Curtis put his hand on John's shoulder. "Sometimes, mental illness can take away our loved ones, John. Personally, I think Jessica was sick, and no one knew it. One day, her mind snapped, and that was that. You should remember her the way she was before all this."

"The last thing I told her was that I hated her, Curtis. I told her to get out, and never come back."

"You didn't hate your daughter, John. You hated the illness that took her away from you."

Curtis shook his hand and watched as John walked back into the house, his shoulders slumped.

CHAPTER SEVENTEEN

The funeral service for Jessica Long was held at 7:00 a.m. on Thursday. It was private and secret, much like Julia Graham's had been eighty years prior. Jessica's sudden and violent death was treated the same way by the locals and was only discussed in hushed tones. Sometimes, it's best to let the dead rest. Curtis did not attend the service.

Steven had taken his DNA test a few days after Jessica's death. It would be a week before the results were known. The little boy was still with his grandparents, who had not left their house, other than to attend the funeral.

Sky Williams called Curtis soon after hearing the news about Jessica. Curtis told him that the diary had been recovered but that he would not be returning it. "But it's my property! You can't keep it! I'll sue you!"

"You can sue if you like, but that diary is a piece of evidence in an ongoing homicide investigation. So it will remain locked up."

"Are you kidding me? What investigation? She killed herself!"

"The case is still open, Sky. Deal with it."

"I need that diary to write, Curtis! I swear I'll get it back! You just wait! You'll be sorry, buddy boy!"

Curtis sighed and hung up the phone. He was pretty certain that Sky was drunk, so he ignored the threats.

The following Monday morning, Curtis met with the DA and Brentley Ford's attorney in Middlebourne. The DA was not agreeable to waiving jail time in exchange for a guilty plea. When the attorney began to argue, the DA threatened to take the case before a grand jury. "Once I get an indictment—and you know I will—the case will go to trial. I have a ninety-three percent success rate in jury trials, so I like my chances."

They finally agreed to thirty days in the county jail and sixty hours of community service in addition to all court costs and fines imposed by the judge. Brentley also promised to repay the victims and insurance companies and signed a sworn statement to that effect.

Curtis left the DA's office and walked across the street to the pizza place. It was owned by the Boggs family, and they served up some of the best pizza in the area. He ordered his favorite, a personal pizza with the works. Curtis made it a point to eat there whenever he was in Middlebourne. After eating, he drove back to Sistersville. When he pulled up to the city building, Steven Andrews was sitting on the front steps, waiting for him.

"What's new, Steven?"

"I'm a dad."

Curtis smiled. "That's awesome! Congratulations!"

"Thanks. I got the results back this morning. I haven't told Marcie yet."

"Why?"

"I don't know. I'm afraid it will freak her out."

"Come on over to my house. Amy is off today. Let's see what she thinks."

The two men walked in through the kitchen door from the garage. Amy was just entering the kitchen from the living room. "Hello, boys! If you're looking for lunch, I haven't started it yet."

"No, babe, we're not. Steven got his DNA test results back. He wanted to talk to you about how to approach Marcie with the news."

Marcie then walked into the kitchen. "Why don't you just tell me?"

"I didn't know you were here, Marcie. I intended to tell you, but I wanted to know how to break the news to you. Curtis suggested that I ask Amy first."

"Well, seeing as how you went all crazy on me last week for not telling *you* the truth right away, I'd say it would be a good idea to tell me now."

"I am the father. The test results confirmed it. The probability is ninety-nine point nine seven."

Marcie sat down at the kitchen table and let out a slow sigh. "Okay then. Where do we go from here?"

"I don't know. What am I supposed to do? I've never been in a situation like this."

Amy grabbed Curtis by the hand and led him into the living room. "So, how do you think the Longs will react? That's his kid. Shouldn't he be the one raising it now?"

"Lord, Amy, I don't know. How will Marcie react to raising someone else's kid? That's all he's worried about right now."

"Well, Marcie and I have been talking about this possibility for days, and she's open to the thought of raising Junior."

"She is?"

"Yes. We talked about it, and we agreed that if Junior was Steven's son, then he was a part of him. With Jessica gone, the boy needs a mother. Can you think of a better person than Marcie?"

"No, I can't. But I'm surprised that she's willing to raise him."

"Well, we'll see how that goes now that it's a reality. We were discussing their options the other day. The best one they had before was adoption. With adoption, you're both raising someone else's kid, right?"

"Yes."

"In this case, they're raising *his* child. That's very different."

"If you say so, I'll agree," he laughed. "Is that what you call female logic?"

"Yes, it *is* logic. Someday, I'll teach it to you."

"That's funny, Amy! But shouldn't we be checking on the kids in our kitchen?"

They walked back into the kitchen to find Marcie and Steven kissing. Curtis gave Amy a hug and laughed. "See? We can't leave them alone for a minute!"

CHAPTER EIGHTEEN

A few weeks went by, and life was returning to normal for Curtis Knight. He attended the hearing for Bentley Ford, mainly to see the look on Bradly's face when his son stood before the judge and entered a guilty plea. Deep down, Curtis felt the urge to celebrate openly in court, but his professionalism prevented that from happening. When they were leaving the courtroom, Bradly shot a mean glance his way. Curtis smiled back.

Marcie and Steven had worked out a visitation arrangement with the Longs, who were enjoying having their grandson around. It was eventually agreed that the Longs would maintain custody, but Steven would be involved in all aspects of Junior's life from then on. The option to keep the boy full time was just too overwhelming for Marcie and Steven right now. They had discussed it together at length and then with the Longs.

Sky Williams filed a complaint with the DA, requesting that his property be returned. It was denied. His drunken phone calls and threats to

Curtis continued but were growing less frequent each week. Three months later the DA called Curtis and told him the diary could be returned, as he had officially closed the Jessica Long case. But Curtis left it in the evidence locker. He didn't think it was a good idea to return it with Sky drinking so much. The diary was too powerful to be placed in the hands of a drunk.

Thanksgiving came and then Christmas. As Amy entered her ninth month of pregnancy, she cut back on her night shifts and was only working part time. Doc Gwynn was making weekly visits to her house for checkups.

The New Year was approaching. All signs pointed to a happy one for Curtis Knight.

At around 4:00 p.m. on New Year's Eve, Curtis's cell phone rang. He saw Sky's number and almost didn't answer. He was in too good a mood to listen to another drunken tirade. But because he *was* in a good mood, he answered anyway. "Hello, Sky."

"Hey, Curtis! Listen, dude, I want to apologize for all the things I've said to you. I was just frustrated and drunk. I'm actually finishing up a new book and was wondering if you'd mind if I stopped by the police station so you can give it a review."

"Sure. What would be a good time for you?"

"Anytime this evening … unless you have plans?"

"No, Amy is filling in for a friend at the hospital tonight. Swing by around seven."

Curtis was relieved to hear that his friend was writing again. He knew it had been tough on him not having the diary. But Sky was a natural-born writer, and maybe this would prove to him that he didn't need it anymore.

Sky arrived promptly at 7:00 p.m. He handed Curtis a one-inch-thick, bound manuscript. "This is it. I haven't written the last chapter yet. Actually, I'll need your help to do that."

Curtis took the manuscript and read the title page: *This is the End.*

"I haven't edited it yet; this is just a rough draft. You can keep it; it's a copy."

"Thank you, Sky. I'm looking forward to reading it. What's it about?"

"The diary and all the problems it caused me. Of course, I used a fictional character to be me because no one would believe the truth!"

"So you wrote about yourself but used a fictional character. That's brilliant, Sky!"

Sky laughed. "Well, they say the secret to good writing is writing about what you know best!"

"That's true! So how can I help you write the last chapter? You have me intrigued."

"I want you to destroy the diary."

"Destroy it? Why?"

"My life wasn't great before I found it, Curtis, but it certainly wasn't bad. The diary brought me money and fame, but I haven't been happy. If you gave it back to me, I'd use it again. I don't want to do that."

"What makes you so sure I'd give it back to you?"

"Because all I have to do is ask. I received a letter from the DA two months ago telling me I could claim it."

"So why didn't you?"

"I was writing again. For the first time in two years, I was writing on my own. I didn't need to use the diary. I was free of it."

"And you think my destroying it will free you from future temptation?"

"Yes! Curtis, before I found that thing, I never drank. Afterwards, I was a lush! I was suddenly chasing after loose women and having terrible nightmares. My whole personality changed. I was thinking dark and evil things. A few months ago, I quit drinking, and the nightmares have stopped."

"Then, I'll destroy it for you, Sky."

Curtis walked over to the evidence locker and opened it, removing the diary. He went over to his desk and sat down with it in his hand.

"So how do you want this done?"

Sky walked over to the desk and pulled up a chair alongside Curtis. He inched closer to him and said, "Jessica Long."

"I'm sorry, what?"

"I want you to think about Jessica Long."

At that moment, Sky's right hand shot out, and his fingers grabbed hold of the key in the lock, twisting it before Curtis even realized what was happening. The orange glow flashed throughout the office, and Curtis's body became rigid and still.

Sky grabbed the diary from Curtis's hand and placed it in his pocket. He slid the key in after it. "You're a gullible man, Curtis Knight! You should have listened to me! I said you would pay, didn't I?"

Sky picked up the manuscript and opened it. He held it out toward Curtis as he flipped through the pages. "See? All blank! You didn't even notice!

Well, guess what? You didn't write the last chapter for me; you wrote it for yourself. This *is* the end!"

After walking out of the police station, Sky walked down to the ferry boat landing and tossed the key into the Ohio River. He returned to his house and opened a bottle of vodka. For the next three hours, he sat in his kitchen and drank. At last, he stood up, wobbling a bit, before slowly making his way into the den. He sat at his desk, placed the diary on top of it, and then opened the middle drawer. He pulled out his revolver and placed the barrel against his temple. He looked at the diary and recalled the discussion he'd had with the old woman in Tennessee. As he squeezed the trigger, he whispered, "My terms."

CHAPTER NINETEEN

When rookie cop Rob Hyatt found Curtis unresponsive at 10:45 that night, he called for an ambulance. They transported Curtis to Sistersville General Hospital, where Amy was working. When she saw his eyes, she screamed and fainted.

Steven Andrews and Marcie Johnson arrived at the hospital fifteen minutes later. Doc Gwynn pulled Steven aside. "He appears to be in a coma. But it's unlike anything I've ever seen before. His eyes are devoid of life, almost as if he were dead, yet his heart and lungs are still functioning. His vital signs are perilously low, and I don't know how long he will survive in this state."

The paramedic who had transported Curtis was standing near them and spoke up, "That's the same look that Harriet Long had."

After speaking to her for a few minutes, Steven left the hospital and rushed to the police station. He went inside and checked the evidence locker. The diary was gone. He pulled the evidence log out and checked the owner's name. After radioing Officer Hyatt, Steven ran the half block to Sky Williams' house. The front door was open. He didn't wait for the rookie cop. He found Sky's dead body slumped over in a chair in the den. The diary was lying on the desk.

When Officer Hyatt arrived, Steven instructed him to begin searching for the key. Steven radioed dispatch and requested that the paramedic and EMT who had taken Curtis to the hospital assist him at Sky's house. They had found the key before, and Steven hoped they would help him find it now.

Back at the hospital, Amy was regaining consciousness. She began to scream for Curtis. Doc Gwynn tended to her, but was reluctant to administer a sedative due to her pregnancy. Marcie assisted him as best she could, but it became apparent that Amy was not going to be calmed. "Marcie, go get the cloth wrist restraints," Doc ordered.

Amy lifted her hips high into the air and screamed, "Curtis!"

Her water broke. Doc Gwynn calmly moved to position himself between her legs. He pulled off her scrub pants and panties and tossed them aside. He called out for a nurse to assist him. When

Marcie returned with the restraints, Doc told her to place them on her wrists and tie them to the bed rails while he placed her legs in the stirrups. A nurse entered the room and began talking gently to Amy, instructing her to push with each contraction.

Doc Gwynn was surprised at how quickly Amy had dilated. Considering this was her first child, things were moving rapidly. Suddenly the crown of the baby's head appeared, and Doc reached down to help guide Curtis and Amy Knight's little girl into the world.

Curtis was moved from the ER to an intensive care bed. His condition remained unchanged.

Amy was sedated immediately after she delivered her baby girl.

The search at Sky's house continued.

Doc Gwynn had slept in the nurses' break room overnight. He didn't want to be far from Curtis or Amy. After getting only a few hours of sleep, he awoke and splashed some water on his face. He made his way to the nursery and picked the newborn up from her bassinet. He examined her closely, even though he had checked her immediately after her delivery a few hours before. The baby girl was a healthy 6 lbs. 9 ounces and was

17 inches in length. She had a surprising amount of light brown hair. As he examined her, he noticed the pink birthmark on the back of her neck. It was located just below her hairline. Doc knew that this was the best place to have a birthmark, because as she aged, no one would notice it there. Some folks referred to this type of birthmark as a "stork bite" or "salmon patch." Many believed the old wives' tale that birthmarks were shaped by a traumatic event in the mother's life. Doc scoffed at that idea.

He put the baby down and went to check on Curtis and Amy.

Had he taken a moment to lift the hair on the back of the baby's head, he would have noticed that the entire birthmark had a very distinctive shape. It resembled the shape of a key …

Printed in the United States
By Bookmasters